BABA

BABA

For Holly, Calum, Kieran and Martha

A Red Fox Book

Published by Random House Children's Books
20 Vauxhall Bridge Road, London SW1V 2SA
A division of Random House UK Ltd
London Melbourne Sydney Auckland
Johannesburg and agencies throughout the world

1 3 5 7 9 10 8 6 4 2

First published in Great Britain by Andersen Press Ltd 1997
Red Fox edition 1999

Printed in Hong Kong

RANDOM HOUSE UK Limited Reg. No. 954009

ISBN 0 09 940078 2

BABA

Ruth Brown

RED FOX

We went for a walk one day, my brothers and I. Mum said we had to take our little sister with us. She's such a cry baby. She never goes anywhere without her old comfort blanket. She even talks to it, and when she's upset she hugs it and cries,

"Baba, Baba."

She couldn't climb over the gate,
so she cried, "Baba, Baba."

She was frightened of the cows, so she cried, "Baba, Baba."

She couldn't cross the stream,
so she cried, "Baba, Baba."

She got caught in the brambles, so she cried, "Baba, Baba."

She even started to howl, "Baba, Baba,"
when we were just walking down the lane.
"What are you crying for now?" we shouted.

"Baba, Baba," she sobbed, holding up the very last strand of her blanket. It had totally unravelled.

"It's OK," we said. "Don't cry. We'll wind it up and then it can be knitted again. You'll see - it'll be fine."

But before we could start, our little sister pushed us out of the way.

Winding the wool, she ran up the lane,

tore through the brambles,

jumped over the stream,

marched past the cows,

and climbed the gate.

"Here you are," she said when
we finally caught up with her.
"Catch!"

And we played with the big
woollen ball all the way home,
my brothers, my sister and I.

Some
bestselling Red Fox
picture books

This Little Tiger book
belongs to:

_____

_____

_____

For all those who stay true
in an ever-changing world ~ O H

For Finnley and Jocelyn, may your worlds be full of adventures,
but also include moments of relative calm to enjoy a nice cup of tea and a biscuit ~ S J

LITTLE TIGER PRESS LTD
an imprint of the Little Tiger Group
1 Coda Studios
189 Munster Road
London SW6 6AW
www.littletiger.co.uk

First published in Great Britain 2017
This edition published 2018
Text by Owen Hart
Text copyright © Little Tiger Press 2017
Illustrations copyright © Sean Julian 2017
Sean Julian has asserted his right to be identified
as the illustrator of this work under the Copyright,
Designs and Patents Act, 1988
A CIP catalogue record for this book is available from the British Library
All rights reserved

ISBN 978-1-84869-684-6
Printed in China
LTP/1800/2189/0318
10 9 8 7 6 5 4 3 2 1

I'll Love You For Ever

Owen Hart

Sean Julian

LITTLE TIGER

LONDON

I'll love you for ever.
I'll always be here,
To share in the laughter
of each passing year.

Though seasons may turn,
bringing sights new and strange,
My love is the one thing
that won't ever change.

On crisp winter days
off exploring we'll go.
We'll tumble and leap
through the pretty, white snow.

Come look at this snowflake
and I will explain:
In spring it'll melt
but my love will remain.

We'll both gaze in wonder
as the new shoots peep through.
Each flower that blossoms,
I'll share it with you.

As the days become warmer
we'll fill them with fun –
A splash in the sea,
then a snooze in the sun.

At the end of each day
I will kiss you goodnight
And never grow tired
of holding you tight.

And when the birds tell us
that summer has come,
We'll play in the grass
while the bees gently hum.

The leaves will turn golden
as fall comes along.
The flowers may fade
but my love will stay strong.

When cold, winter winds
blow the leaves far and wide,
You'll cross the great icebergs
with me by your side.

But for now, cuddle close,
watch the stars softly shine.

I'll always be yours
and you'll always be mine.

Through each changing season
and each passing year,
I'll love you for ever
and ever, my dear.

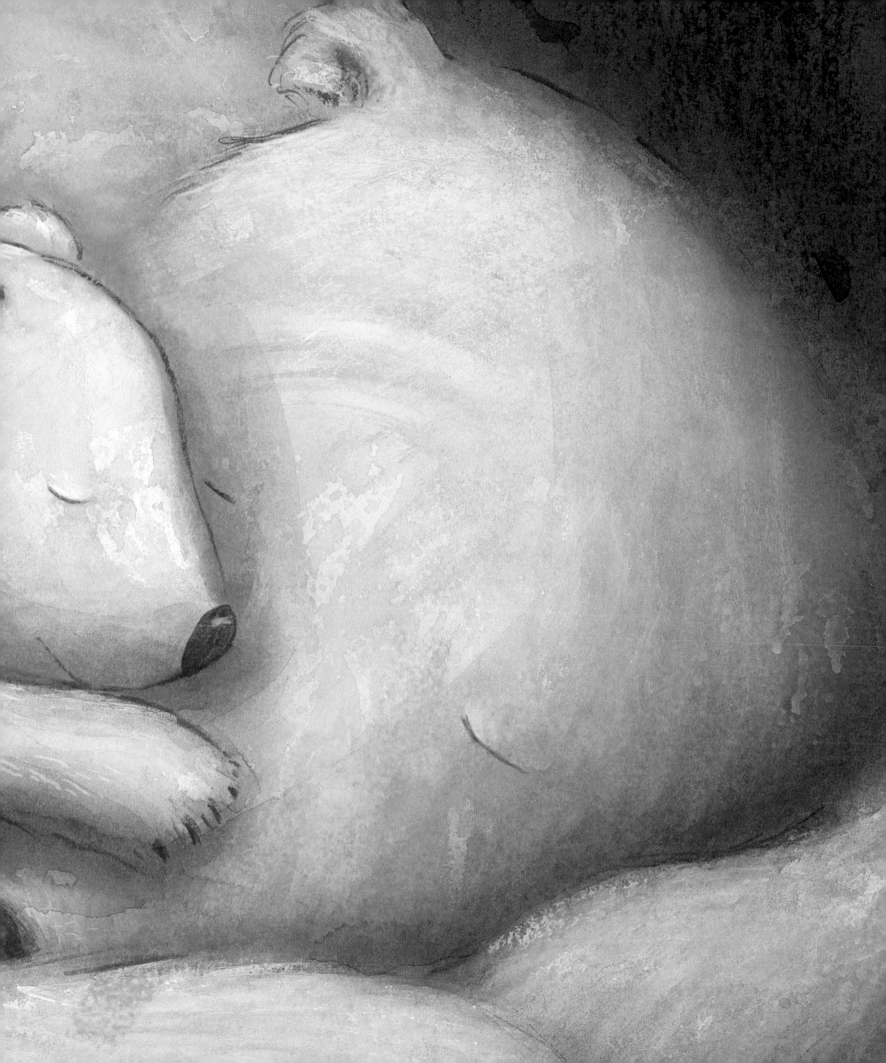